The Runaway Princess

Rosie Dickins
Illustrated by Elodie Coudray

Reading consultant: Alison Kelly
University of Roehampton

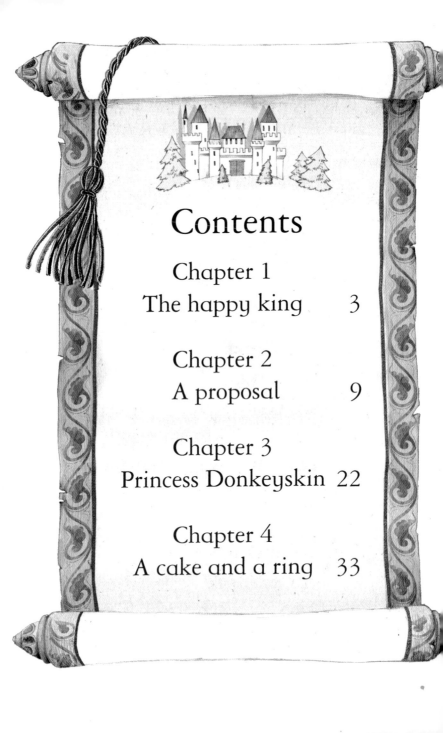

Contents

Chapter 1

The happy king

There was once a happy king. He lived with his queen and her little sister in a magnificent mountain palace.

The palace was filled with
treasures and wonders. The
most wonderful of all was a
magic donkey, who could
turn straw into gold.

But the king's happiness did not last, for his dear queen fell ill. The doctors said she didn't have long to live.

"Promise me something," she begged her husband.

"Anything," vowed the king.
"Don't marry again," she
whispered, "until you find a
wife as good as me!"
And then she died.

Now the king's heart grew cold. As the years went by, people begged him to remarry.

But he always refused.

"There is no one as good as my queen," he snapped.

And so he grew old and cruel, with only Anna, the queen's sister, for company.

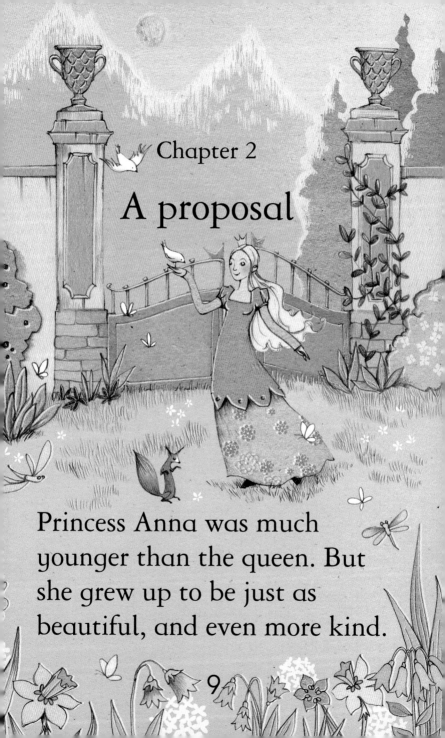

Chapter 2

A proposal

Princess Anna was much younger than the queen. But she grew up to be just as beautiful, and even more kind.

In time, even the king
noticed how lovely she was.
"Now I can keep my promise,"
he decided.

Anna's heart sank. She couldn't marry this cruel old man, but she was too afraid to tell him. Then she had an idea.

I'll set him an impossible task!

"I could never marry without a dress as beautiful as the sky," she said.

The king snapped his fingers. "Fetch my best dressmakers," he ordered.

That night, the king gave Anna a dress of shimmering blue, embroidered all over with silky clouds.

Anna thought quickly. "Not without a dress as beautiful as the moon," she replied.

Again, the king snapped his fingers. "Get those dressmakers back here!" he said.

The next day, there was a
dress of shining silver, trimmed
with glowing moonstones.

"Not without a dress as beautiful as the sun," pleaded the poor princess.

So the king snapped his fingers again...

The next day, there was
a dress of glittering gold,
scattered with scarlet rubies.

Anna was in despair. "There's one more thing," she pleaded. "I'd like a cloak of donkey skin. And not any old skin. It must be from a magic donkey!"

The next day, the king presented Anna with a shaggy donkeyskin cloak.

"We'll be married tomorrow," he told her.

Anna bowed her head.
"There's only one thing left to
do," she decided. "Run away!"

When the king was in bed, she
bundled up her dresses, put on
the cloak and crept downstairs.

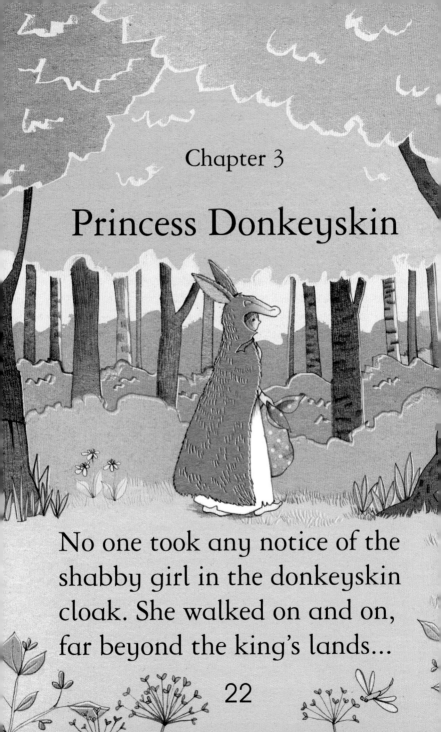

Chapter 3

Princess Donkeyskin

No one took any notice of the shabby girl in the donkeyskin cloak. She walked on and on, far beyond the king's lands...

...until she came to a farmhouse by a forest.

The farmer's wife looked curiously at Anna. "What's your name?" she asked. Anna didn't answer.

"I'll call you Donkeyskin," laughed the woman. "If you're looking for work, we need a girl to look after the geese."

Donkeyskin worked hard.
The farmer and his wife
grew very fond of her. They
never guessed their goose girl
was a runaway princess.

Sometimes, as she herded the geese, Anna heard hunting horns in the forest. One day, she spotted a handsome prince among the trees.

That evening, she hid in her room and took out the sky-blue dress...

The prince was riding home
when he spotted the farmhouse.
"I'll stop and ask for a drink,"
he decided.

One of the windows glowed with a mysterious blue light. Inside, the prince saw a girl in a shimmering blue dress.

"She's as beautiful as the sky," he thought, losing his heart to her.

The next day, the prince sent a messenger to the farm. But there was no sign of a girl in a sky-blue dress.

Chapter 4

A cake and a ring

The prince sent out messengers far and wide. None of them could find the mystery girl.

Hoping against hope, the prince rode back to the farm. This time, a silver light shone from one of the windows. His heart leaped.

The girl was in the kitchen,
dressed in shining silver.
"She's as beautiful as
the moon," sighed
the prince.

He knocked eagerly, then
opened the door.

Quick as a flash, Anna hid, leaving a cake cooling on the table.

It smelled so good, the prince couldn't help taking a bite. It was deliciously sweet and soft...

...and then his teeth crunched on something hard.

He spat out a tiny gold ring. "It's hers," he realized. "It must have fallen off while she was cooking."

The ring gave the prince an idea. He galloped back to his castle to make a royal decree.

Hundreds of girls came to try the ring, from countesses to chambermaids. It didn't fit any of them.

Anna stood at the back of
the great hall, wrapped in her
donkeyskin cloak.

"Is there anyone else?" asked the prince eventually.

"Just that girl in the shabby cloak," laughed a courtier.

The prince looked into
Anna's eyes. "Let her try the
ring," he insisted.

The courtier frowned.

Anna held out her hand.
The ring was a perfect fit.
 "Will you marry me?" asked
the prince.

"Yes," said Anna, letting the
cloak slip from her shoulders.
Everyone gasped.

43

Her dress shone with gold
and rubies, filling the hall
with golden light. But her
golden hair and rosy cheeks
shone even brighter.

"She's as beautiful as the sun," sighed the courtiers.

The prince smiled at Anna. "I knew I'd find you," he whispered happily.

The wedding was held a few days later. The prince invited royal guests from around the world. Anna invited the kind farmer and his wife.

Anna told their guests her whole story...

"But now I'll never run away again!" she finished, gazing joyfully at her prince.

About the story

The Runaway Princess is a very old fairy tale. In some versions, the princess has a cloak made of rags or all kinds of fur. This retelling is based on *Donkeyskin*, a 300-year-old story by the French writer Charles Perrault.

Designed by Caroline Spatz
Series editor: Lesley Sims

First published in 2013 by Usborne Publishing Ltd., Usborne House, 83-85 Saffron Hill, London EC1N 8RT, England. www.usborne.com
Copyright © 2013 Usborne Publishing Ltd.